Bloomsbury Publishing, London, New Delhi, New York and Sydney

First published in Great Britain in December 2014 by Bloomsbury Publishing Plc
50 Bedford Square, London WC1B 3DP

Published by arrangement with TOON BOOKS/RAW Junior, LLC,
27 Greene Street, New York, NY 10013

www.bloomsbury.com

Bloomsbury is a registered trademark of Bloomsbury Publishing Plc

A CIP catalogue record for this book is available from the British Library

ISBN 978 1 4088 6198 1

Book design by Françoise Mouly and Jonathan Bennett
Printed in China by C&C Offset Printing Co Ltd, Shenzhen, Guangdong

1 3 5 7 9 10 8 6 4 2

NEIL GAIMAN

LORENZO MATTOTTI

Hansel & Gretel

BLOOMSBURY

LONDON NEW DELHI NEW YORK SYDNEY

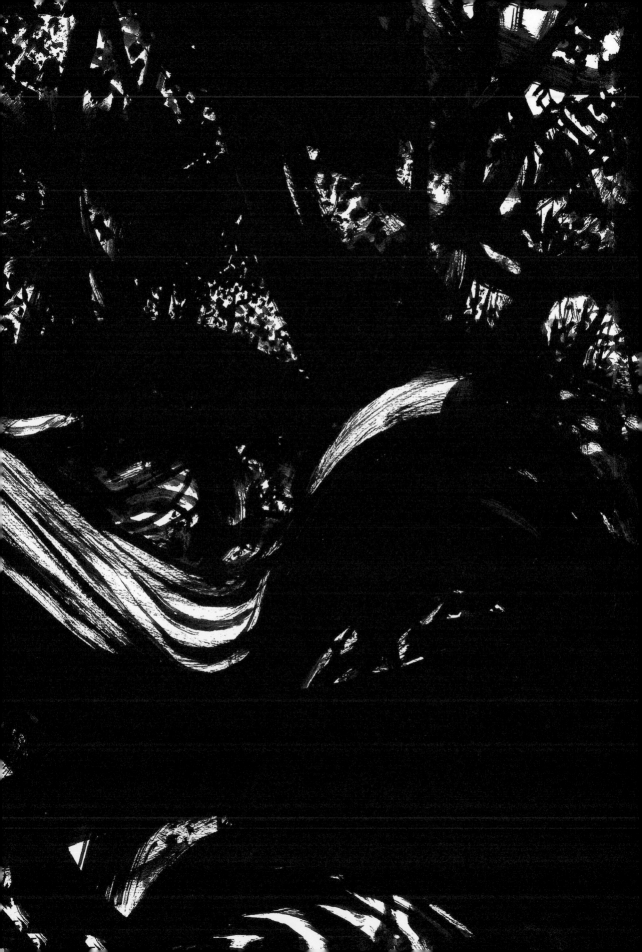

This all happened a long time ago, in your grandmother's time, or in her grandfather's. A long time ago. Back then, we all lived on the edge of the great forest.

There was a woodcutter. He cut down trees. He chopped the branches off the trees, and he cut the trunks and the branches into logs for firewood, which he would haul on a handcart to the nearest path into the town. It was hungry work, cutting trees.

The woodcutter took a pretty young wife, who helped him as best she could. She cooked for him, and she gave him every comfort, so it was no surprise to them that, shortly after they were married, her belly began to swell and, in the winter, when the snows were high, she gave birth to a girl. The child was called Margaret, which they shortened to Greta, and then to Gretel. Two years later the woodcutter's wife gave birth to a boy, and they called him Hans, which, because they could make it no shorter, they made longer and changed to Hansel.

Hansel and Gretel did not go to school, for the schools

were far from the forest where they lived, and schools cost money, which the woodcutter did not have enough of, for you do not make much money from hewing wood and hauling logs. Even so, their father taught them the way of the woods, and their mother taught them how to cook and to clean and to sew. And if their mother was sometimes bitter and sharp-tongued, and if their father was sometimes sullen and eager to be away from their little home, why, Gretel and Hansel thought nothing of it, as long as they could play in the forest, and climb trees and ford rivers; as long as there were freshly baked bread and eggs and cooked cabbage on their table.

When the wood sold well, their father would buy meat for the family at the market: a fat-tailed sheep or a goat, which he would bring back trotting behind his hand-drawn cart; or even a hunk of raw beef, dripping with blood, black with flies or yellow with wasps, and the family would feast that evening. There were rabbits in the forest, there were ducks in the woodcutter's pond, there were chickens scratching in the dirt behind the woodcutter's tiny house. There was always food.

That was in the good days, before the war, before the famine.

War came, and the soldiers came with it—hungry, angry, bored, scared men who, as they passed through, stole the cabbages and the chickens and the ducks. The woodcutter's family was never certain who was fighting whom, nor why they were fighting, nor what they were fighting about. But beyond the forest, fields of crops were burned and barley fields became battlefields, and the farmers were killed, or made into soldiers in their turn and marched away. And soon enough the miller had no grain to mill into flour, the butcher had no animals to kill and hang in his window, and they said you could name your own price for a fat rabbit.

Soon enough, the root vegetables rotted in the fields, all the turnips and carrots and potatoes, for there were fewer and fewer people to dig them up. And it rained and it rained, so the only things to eat their fill, in those fields, were the slugs.

The woodcutter's cottage was far from the battles, but the

woodcutter, and his wife, and Gretel, and Hansel, all felt the war's effect. They ate soup made from old cabbage leaves, into which the children would dip their stale bread, now hard as a stone, and the family went to bed hungry and woke up hungrier.

The children slept on straw pallets. Their parents slept in an ancient bed that had once belonged to the woodcutter's grandmother. Hansel woke in the night, a sharp, empty pain in his stomach, but he did not say anything, for he knew there was little enough to eat. He kept his eyes closed and tried to return to sleep. When he slept, he was not hungry.

He could hear his parents talking in the darkness.

"There are four of us," his mother was saying. "Four mouths to feed. If we keep going like this, we'll all die. Without the extra mouths, you and I will have a chance."

"We cannot," replied the woodcutter, in a whisper. "It would be a monstrous thing to do, to kill our children, and I will have no part of it."

"*Lose* them, not *kill* them," said the woodcutter's wife.

"Nobody said anything about killing anybody. We'll take them deep into the forest, and lose them. They will be fine. Perhaps a kind person will take them in, and feed them. And we can always have more children," she added, practically.

"A bear might eat them," said the woodcutter, dejectedly. "We cannot do this thing."

"If you do not eat," said his wife, "then you will not be able to swing an axe. And if you cannot cut down a tree, or haul the wood into the town, then we all starve and die. Two dead are better than four dead. That is mathematics, and it is logic."

"I care for neither your mathematics nor your logic," grumbled the woodcutter. "But I can argue no more."

And Hansel heard only silence from his parents' bed.

Gretel woke Hansel the next morning. "It is going to be a good day," she said. "Our father is going to take us into the forest with him, and he will teach us to cut wood." Their father would not ordinarily take them with him deep into the forest. He said it was too dangerous for children.

Hansel went down to the little stream that splashed and sang behind their cottage, and he filled his pockets with the tiny white stones that lined the stream bed.

"Why are you doing that?" asked Gretel.

Hansel looked up and saw his parents standing by the doorway, and he said nothing to his sister. Their father took them into the forest. At each turn they took, Hansel quietly dropped a little white stone to mark each change of direction.

Their father told them to wait for him in a grove of birch trees, their trunks paper-white against the darkness of the forest. He built them a small fire, to keep them warm.

He gave them his lunch to keep them from hunger: stale black bread and hard cheese.

He would be back for them soon, he said.

They waited.

"He is never coming back," said Hansel.

"He is our father," said Gretel. "You must not say such things about him."

The day waned and twilight fell, and the shadows crept out from beneath each tree and puddled and pooled until the world was one huge shadow.

"He is not coming back for us," said Hansel.

"We must wait," said Gretel. "Perhaps he is delayed."

She gathered a pile of leaves, and the two children made themselves as comfortable as they could beside the crackling fire.

They awoke in the small hours of the night, when the fire was only embers. The moon was full, and in the moon's light Hansel found it easy to retrace his steps: the white stones from the stream were perfectly visible even in the darkness. Hansel and Gretel held hands as they walked.

It was almost dawn when they returned to the cottage. Their father's face was crimson, and his eyes were red and wet, as if he had been crying and drinking. When he saw them, he jumped up. "It is Hansel!" he exclaimed. "And it is Gretel! We thought you were lost in the forest.

But look, wife! Look at them! Our children are here!"

Their mother's face was pale, and her lips were thin, and she watched them, and said nothing.

The woodcutter hugged them tightly to him, and he cried and he laughed and he cried and he laughed once more, and he gave the children each a swollen cherry soaked in syrup, from a jar that had once been filled with them and was now almost empty, to show them both how pleased he was that they were home.

Their mother looked hungrily at the last four cherries in the jar.

The children sucked on the cherries as long as they could, making them last, before they swallowed them.

The children stayed in the house for another week, and a week after that, and nothing was said about the time they were lost in the forest and found their way home again. Hansel would lie there, in the night, awake, listening in the darkness, but he heard nothing but snores and rustles.

And then, one morning, their father announced he was taking them with him to work.

Hansel was not prepared: there was no time to go to the stream, no time to fill his pockets with white stones. Their mother had been up early baking with the last of the flour, and as they made ready to walk into the forest, she came over to them, two small loaves of white bread in her apron, soft and hot from the oven.

The children followed their father into the deep forest, past trees that tangled together like clutching hands, with fingers that scrapped and scraped.

Hansel had no pebbles, but he made little balls of bread between his fingers and dropped them at each intersection, and each time they changed direction, to mark the way.

They reached a river, and their father showed them where to ford it, where the river was shallow and the rocks stuck up from the water. They took off their shoes, and they carried them until they reached the far bank, where the trees were thick, and old, and gnarled into shapes that looked like angry giants, frozen into time.

They went so deep into the old forest that the sunlight was stained green by the leaves. They pushed through brambles, and the thorns tugged at their clothes as if to say "Stay here! Stay here!"

But they plunged deeper into the forest.

Finally, their father said, "Wait here for me. I'll be back for you," and he turned, and he walked away. They heard him pushing through the thicket, and then they heard nothing more.

"He is not coming back for us," said Gretel.

"No," agreed Hansel.

They were so hungry. Gretel divided her little loaf into two, and she shared it with her brother. The daylight began to fade. They talked about what they could do, and where they could go, but the only place they knew was their home.

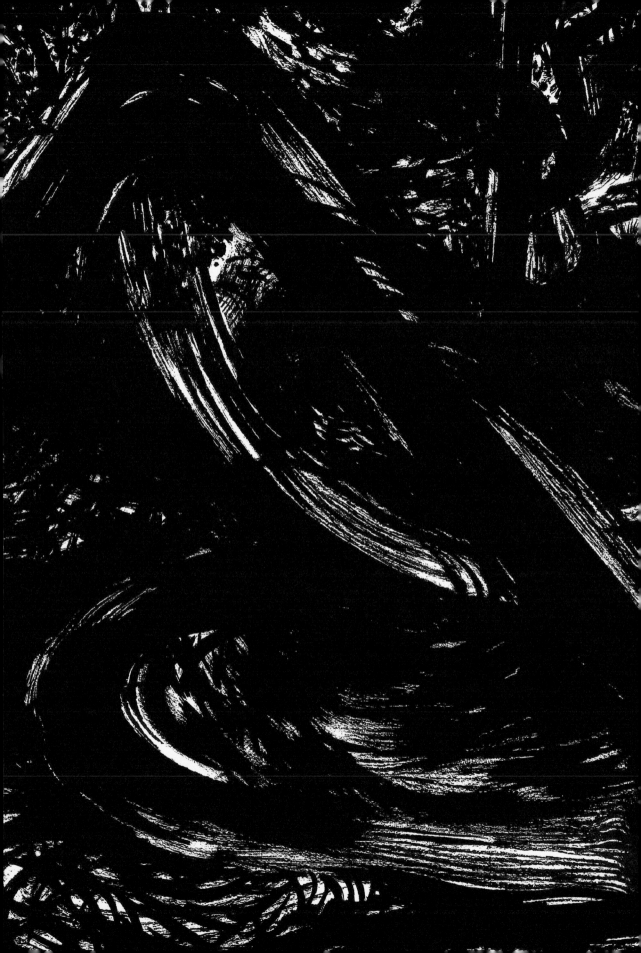

At the first place where Hansel remembered that he had dropped a little bread ball, they stopped. He looked on the ground to see which way they should go, but the bread ball had gone.

"I think we came this way," said Gretel. But she was not certain. They went that way.

"At the bottom of this hill," said Hansel, "I left another bread ball."

But there was nothing at the bottom of the hill, only a wood pigeon pecking at the remaining crumbs of bread. It flew off when it saw the children.

"The creatures of the forest are hungry too," said Gretel.

Hansel said nothing. He knew he could not find his way back without his clues: one tree, one hill, one gnarled root, one stream, all look very much like another.

They walked until it grew too dark to see, and they slept beneath a huge oak tree in a bed they made of mounded-up leaves. And they were cold, and sad, and scared of bears and of wolves and other things in the forest that might eat children.

Morning came. "I am cold, and I am hungry," said Hansel. Gretel hugged her brother tightly.

"We must go home," said Gretel. "Our parents will be worried about us."

Hansel did not reply. He had smelled something on the morning air. Something as sweet and as warm and as wholesome and heartening as...

"Gingerbread!" he told his sister. "I smell gingerbread."

"You smell nothing."

"Sniff the air!" said Hansel.

She sniffed. Freshly baked gingerbread: now even Gretel could smell it. Her mouth watered, and her stomach began to hurt, as if it had just remembered that it was there.

They walked towards the smell: honey cake, and ginger and spices, a glorious sweetness that stole over them. Now the children ran toward the source of the smell, impelled by hunger, going in a direction they had never been before, until, in a clearing, they saw a tiny house, even smaller than their own.

"Someone in that house must be baking," said Gretel.

But she was wrong. The smell came from the house itself. It was made of fresh gingerbread, decorated with hard sugar candies of green and red. Even the windows were clear panes of barley sugar. Hansel reached out and broke off a window ledge. Gretel hesitated, but when she saw her brother eating and smiling, she pulled off a shingle from the wall, and they ate together, letting the spicy gingerbread fill their mouths, their heads, their stomachs.

A voice from inside, gentle and amused: "Who nibbles my house? Is it a mouse?" Hansel and Gretel said nothing, for they were scared, and their mouths were full, and they were relieved when the person who came out of the little house was not an ogre or a monster, but a kindly-faced old woman, leaning on a stick, who peered about her shortsightedly with dim eyes.

"Why, you're children!" she said. "You must be so hungry, children, to eat my house like that. Come in, come inside, and let me feed you!"

There was only one room in the little house, with a huge brick oven at one end, and a table laden with all good things: with candied fruits, with cakes and pies and cookies, with breads and with biscuits. There was no meat, though, and the old woman apologised, explaining that she was old, and her eyes were not what they had been when she was young, and she was no longer up to catching the beasts of the forests, as once she had been. Now, she told the children, she baited her snare and she waited, and often no game would come to her trap from one year to another, and what she did catch was too scrawny to eat and needed to be fattened up first.

"Still," she said, "you children give me hope, and I think it is lucky that you have come. Perhaps now there will be meat once again."

The children told her of their mother and their father, and how they had been taken into the forest and abandoned, and the old woman tutted and clucked and shook her head.

"Whatever is the world coming to?" she said sadly, and

she showed the children to their little beds, the sheets so white and crisp, the pillows so soft.

They slept as deeply and as soundly as if their food had been drugged. And it had.

The old woman was stronger than she looked—a sinewy, gristly strength: she picked Hansel up, and carried the sleeping boy into the empty stable at the rear of the little house, where there was a large metal cage with rusty bars. She dropped him onto the straw, for there was only straw on the floor, along with a few ancient and well-chewed bones, and she locked the cage, and she felt her way along the wall, back to her house.

"Meat," she said, happily.

Gretel awoke in a dark corner of the cottage, on the floor. The little beds had been removed, as had the uneaten food that had been left on the table. She was tied to the table leg by a long chain.

There was nothing sweet about the old woman, not any longer. She made Gretel clean and work for her, and if the

girl did not obey her fast enough she would beat her and call her all manner of evil names.

And each day the old woman would hobble out to the stable, and she would go to the bars of the cage, and she would tell Hansel to hold out a finger for her to feel, so she could see if he was fattening up to her liking.

She fed him cake and she fed him potatoes and candied fruit. She fed him puddings of all kinds, and fools and gruels and crumbles and cobblers. She would stand beside the cage as he ate, listening to make sure that he swallowed every crumb, licked every bowl clean, and she would poke at him with her stick if he dared to complain that he was full, that he could not choke down another mouthful.

Gretel, chained in the house, could not see her brother, could only hope that he was all right. Sometimes, when she returned from visiting Hansel, the old woman would be in good spirits and she would tell Gretel that she would take care of her and protect her as she grew into a woman, that she would teach the girl all her secrets, teach her to call the birds down from the trees, teach her to ensnare travellers,

to make sure that anyone who came to the cottage would never leave. But an hour later, she would be scolding Gretel, and telling her she was good for nothing at all.

Now, as day followed day, the old woman would return from visiting Hansel in ever-worsening humour.

In truth, Hansel grew fat, but the old woman was too blind to see it. Each day, she reached for his finger, but instead he would hold out a bone he had found in the straw. She felt the bone and, thinking it was the boy's finger, left him for another day. Her patience, however, was not inexhaustible.

One morning, a month or more after the children had been captured, the old woman returned from visiting Hansel, and told Gretel to light a fire in the brick oven.

"Today, when the oven is hot enough, we will roast your brother," said the old woman. "But do not be sad. I will give you his bones to chew, little one."

Gretel shrugged. She hardly spoke to the old woman, only a word or two if she had to. The old woman had begun to suspect that the girl was little more than a half-wit.

Gretel did as she was told. She lit the wood in the oven, watched the branches flare and burn. She closed the door to the oven. Inside the wood was burning. Soon, it would collapse to glowing embers.

"See if it is hot enough to roast your brother yet," said the old woman. "Climb inside and tell me."

"I don't know how," said Gretel, and she stood where she was, making no move even to open the oven door.

"It is easy. Simply open the door, and lean in, and feel if it is hot enough yet to roast flesh."

"I don't know how," said Gretel again.

"You are a slattern and a dolt!" exclaimed the old woman. "Idiot child. I will show you." The old woman hobbled over to the oven, leaning on her stick. "Learn from me." The old woman opened the oven door.

retel had learned more from her than the old woman suspected. The girl pushed the old woman forward, hard and sudden, making her topple all the way into the oven. The girl closed the door, and held it closed, and listened while the old woman's screams died away.

Gretel stared at the oven door, scared that the old woman would somehow survive, that she would open the door and come after her, but nothing happened.

Gretel found the old woman's keys hidden beneath her pillow. She unlocked her chain, and then she went out to the stable.

"The old woman is dead," Gretel told her brother, as she let him out of the cage. "I killed her."

She helped him out of the cage, and out into the daylight, marvelling at the plump young man her brother had transformed into, wondering about his refusal to let go of the bone he held as firmly as if his life might have depended upon it.

They clung to each other tightly, in the sunshine, the brother and the sister.

The kitchen smelled of burning flesh, but when the oven cooled, and they opened the door, there was nothing inside but a blackened husk, now crisped and turned to carbon, and a small iron key.

The key opened a chest beneath the old woman's bed, in which the two children found all manner of things: gloves and hats of travellers, and coins of gold and of silver, a string of pearls, chains of gold and chains of silver, rings set with diamonds and rings set with rubies—all the treasures of the people who had visited the old woman's cottage over the years, and who had never left. There were rich clothes, too, clothes of silks and of satins, trimmed with lace and gold brocade, clothes for men, and fine dresses for women.

The children put on garments from the chest, for their own clothes were rags. They filled a sack with coins and jewellery and precious stones, and they left that place without looking back.

The children walked south, until they came to a river. They forded the river where it was shallow, and soon enough

they recognised the familiar places where they had played, and trees they had climbed.

They walked a path they had known all their lives, and they found themselves in front of the little house in which they had been born.

They called out, not daring to come too close.

The woodcutter ran to meet them. He threw down his axe and embraced them, holding them tightly. He told them he had not been happy for a single day since the children had gone, had not once slept the night through. Each day he had searched for them in the forest, and each day he had failed to find them.

"And our mother?" asked Hansel. "Where is our mother? We have brought precious stones and all manner of riches, and now our mother can eat whatever she wants, and live wherever she wants, and she will not have to be afraid that we will all starve."

The woodcutter said nothing, but he showed them the grave in the garden that he had dug himself for their mother, for she had died soon after the children had gone, whether of something eating her away from inside, or from hunger, or from anger, or loss of her children, no one alive can say.

Hansel and Gretel and their father the woodcutter lived happily in the little house for years to come. The treasures they had brought from the old woman's cottage kept them comfortable, and there were to be no more empty plates in their lives.

In the years that followed, Hansel and Gretel each married, and married well, and the people who went to their weddings ate so much fine food that their belts burst and the fat from the meat ran down their chins, while the pale moon looked down kindly on them all.

 **THE END**

–Neil Gaiman, 2014

HANSEL AND GRETEL...

When French emperor Napoleon invaded their small German kingdom in 1806, the brothers Wilhelm and Jacob Grimm began collecting local fairy tales as a way to defy cultural domination by the French. They transcribed the stories told to them by acquaintances and neighbours, including a twelve-year-old girl, Henriette Dorothea Wild, called Dortchen. It was Dortchen who shared the story of Hansel and Gretel with the Brothers Grimm.

Dortchen's cruel father forbade his six daughters from visiting the Grimm brothers because they were too poor to associate with, so Dortchen had to meet with Wilhelm in secret. Once she grew up, Dortchen was forced to stay home to care for her aging parents, even after her sisters had all married. It was only after her father died, when she was thirty-two, that she became Mrs Grimm. She and Wilhelm were wed in 1825.

"Hansel and Gretel" was first published in 1812, in the Grimms' first collection of German fairy tales, *Children's and Household Tales*. Historians believe the story may have originated during medieval times, when the Great Famine of 1315 drove ordinary people to abandon their children and eat human flesh. In Dortchen's original version, both parents agree to abandon Hansel and Gretel. In the Grimms' later revisions, it is the mother who comes up with the plan, and who seems to care little about the fate of her children. By the seventh edition published in 1857, the mother had become a stepmother, while the father was portrayed in a gentler, kinder light, reluctant to abandon his children but unable to stand up to his wicked wife. Other late additions include a friendly duck that helps the siblings cross the river after their escape.

Like many fairy tales, "Hansel and Gretel" is rich in symbolic significance. The bone that Hansel uses to trick the old woman, for example, represents strength, as bone is one of the body's most permanent parts, so careful readers can trust that Hansel will likely survive his capture. The old woman's manner of death illustrates the enormity of her evil; burning was the common way of executing witches, while superstition held that iron, like the door of the oven, had the power to guard against evil spirits.

Other folk tales from all around the world echo the themes of "Hansel and Gretel." As scary as it is, cannibalism is not unique to this story. In the original "Snow White," the evil queen wants to eat Snow White's lungs and liver after she's killed, while in the first version of "Sleeping Beauty," another evil queen tries to serve the king his son and daughter in a stew.

Arthur Rackham, "Hansel and Gretel," 1909, *The Fairy Tales of the Brothers Grimm*

...A Changing Tale

A hundred years before the Brothers Grimm, French author and fairy-tale collector Charles Perrault recorded "Le petit Poucet," or "Hop-o'-My-Thumb." Hop-o'-My-Thumb, the smallest and cleverest of seven brothers, is also born to woodcutters who put the children out due to famine. Like Hansel, he uses trails of pebbles then breadcrumbs to find his way. The brothers stumble upon the house of an ogre who vows to kill and eat them, but Hop-o'-My-Thumb tricks him into slitting his daughters' throats instead (by swapping their caps). By the end of the story, Hop-o'-My-Thumb ends up with the ogre's money.

In "Nennillo and Nennella", an Italian folk tale, a cruel stepmother demands that a brother and sister be put out of the house. The father leaves them a trail of oats, hoping they can find their way back, but a donkey eats the oats. The children get separated– Nennillo is discovered and brought up by a prince, while Nennella is adopted by a pirate, lost in a shipwreck, and swallowed by a giant fish. Years later, Nennella is reunited with her brother and father, and the prince punishes the stepmother for her cruelty.

In his telling of "Hansel and Gretel," Neil Gaiman never names the old woman as a witch, but fairy-tale precedent leads readers to that suspicion. Wicked witches in the form of old women are everywhere in folk literature: there's Russia's cannibalistic Baba Yaga, who takes in a boy and a girl sent by their stepmother to be her servants. The witch promises not to eat them only if they can complete impossible tasks, like using a sieve to fill a tub of water. The children show kindness to the animals around the house, and, in return, the animals help the children to complete their tasks and escape.

In 1893, Engelbert Humperdinck adapted "Hansel and Gretel" into a children's opera. An instant hit, the opera is frequently performed around the world (often during the Christmas season), though unlike the Grimms' version, it leaves out the parents' abandonment of their children, making for a lighter tale.

In 1819, the Grimms published a small edition of *Children's and Household Tales* specifically for children and asked their brother Ludwig to illustrate it. In 2007, Lorenzo Mattotti continued that tradition by creating the drawings in our book for an exhibit co-curated by TOON Books' Françoise Mouly to celebrate the Metropolitan Opera's staging of Hansel and Gretel. Mattotti's art in turn provided the inspiration for Neil Gaiman's haunting story.

_____

A SHORT BIBLIOGRAPHY:

The Complete Fairy Tales of the Brothers Grimm; Jacob & Wilhelm Grimm. 1812. *The classic stories, penned by the brothers Grimm.*

The Annotated Brothers Grimm; Jacob & Wilhem Grimm and Maria Tatar. W. W. Norton & Co, 2004. *Celebrates and redefines the Grimm canon.*

The Brothers Grimm: From Enchanted Forests to the Modern World; Jack Zipes. Palgrave Macmillan, 2002. *An exposé on the popular romantic notion of the brothers as travelling fableists.*

Clever Maids: The Secret History of the Grimm Fairy Tales; Valerie Paradiz. Basic Books, 2009. *The true story of the forgotten women narrators of the beloved Grimm tales.*

Fairy Tales from the Brothers Grimm; Philip Pullman. Viking Penguin, 2012. *A new English version by the acclaimed author of* His Dark Materials.

www.surlalunefairytales.com
An archive of annotated fairy tales with historical context.